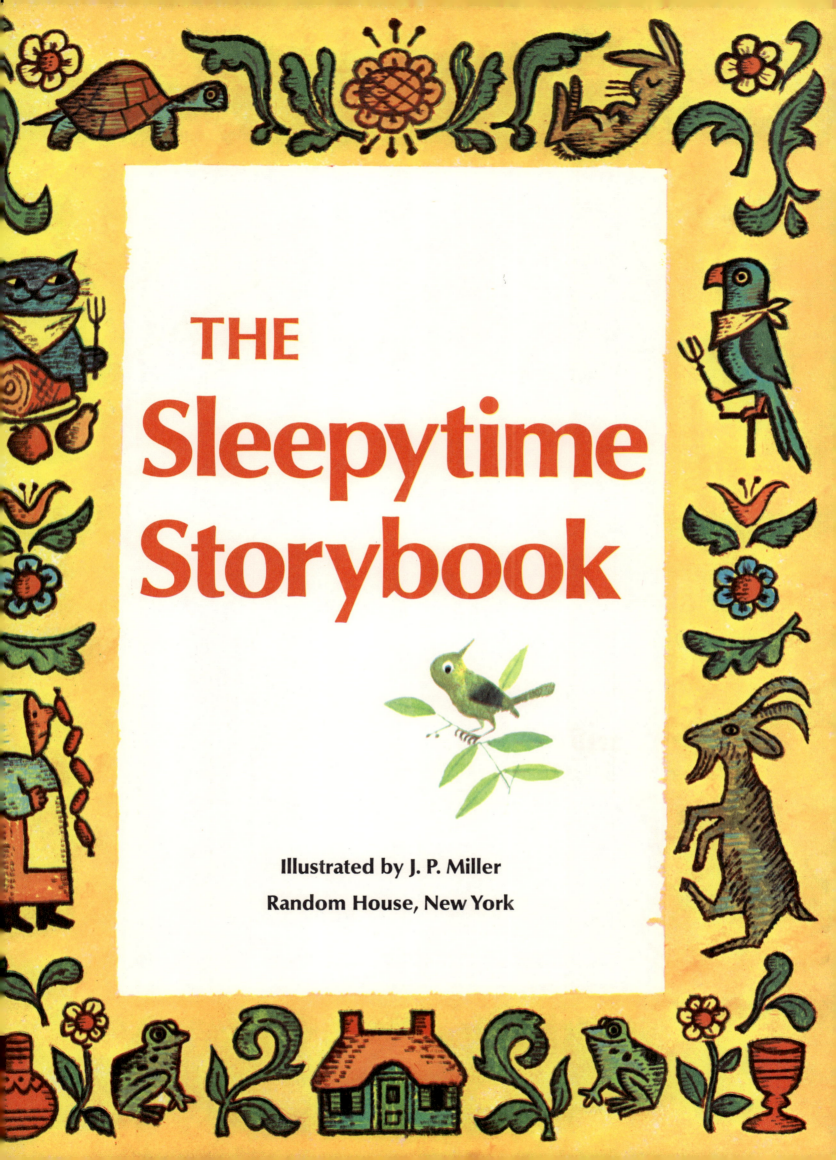

THE
Sleepytime
Storybook

Illustrated by J. P. Miller

Random House, New York

CONTENTS

THE CAT AND THE PARROT

Once there was a cat and a parrot who had agreed to ask each other to dinner, turn and turn about: first the cat should ask the parrot, then the parrot should invite the cat, and so on. It was the cat's turn first.

Now the cat was very mean. He provided nothing at all for dinner except a pint of milk, a little slice of fish, and a biscuit. The parrot was too polite to complain, but he did not have a very good time.

When it was his turn to invite the cat, he cooked a fine dinner. He had a roast of meat, a pot of tea, a basket of fruit, and, best of all, he baked a whole clothesbasketful of little cakes!—little, brown, crispy, spicy cakes! Oh, I should say as many as five hundred. And he put four hundred and ninety-eight of the cakes be-

fore the cat, keeping only two for himself.

Well, the cat ate the roast, and drank the tea, and sucked the fruit, and then he began on the pile of cakes. He ate all the four hundred and ninety-eight cakes, and then he looked around and said: "I'm hungry; haven't you anything else to eat?"

"Why," said the parrot, "here are my two cakes, if you want them."

The cat ate up the two cakes, and then he licked his chops and said, "I am beginning to get an appetite; have you anything else to eat?"

"Well, really," said the parrot, who was now rather angry. "I don't see anything more, unless you wish to eat me!" He thought the cat would be ashamed when he heard that—but the cat just looked at him and licked his chops again—and slip! slop! gobble! down his throat went the parrot!

Then the cat started down the street. An old woman was standing by, and she had seen the whole thing. She was shocked that the cat should eat his friend. "Why, cat!" she said, "how dreadful of you to eat your friend the parrot!"

"Parrot, indeed!" said the cat. "What's a parrot to me? I've a great mind to eat you, too." And—before you could say "Jack Robinson"—slip! slop! gobble! down went the old woman!

Then the cat started down the road again, walking happily, because he felt so fine. Pretty soon he met a man driving a donkey. The man was beating the donkey, to hurry him up, and when he saw the cat he said, "Get out of my way, cat; I'm in a hurry and my donkey might tread on you."

"Donkey, indeed!" said the cat, "much I care for a donkey! I have eaten five hundred cakes, I've eaten my friend the parrot, I've eaten an old woman—what's to hinder my eating a miserable man and a donkey?"

And slip! slop! gobble! down went the old man and the donkey.

Then the cat went on down the road, walking jauntily. After a little, he met a procession, coming that way. The king was at the head, walking proudly with his newly married bride, and behind him were his soldiers, marching, and behind them were ever and ever so many elephants, walking two by two. The king felt very kindly toward everybody, because he had just been married, and he said to the cat, "Get out of my way, pussy, get out of my way—my elephants might hurt you."

"Hurt me!" said the cat, shaking his fat sides. "Ho, ho! I've eaten five hundred cakes, I've eaten my friend the parrot, I've eaten an old woman, I've eaten a man and a donkey; what's to hinder my eating a beggarly king?"

And slip! slop! gobble! down went the king; down went the queen; down went the soldiers—and down went all the elephants!

Then the cat went on, more slowly; he had really had enough to eat, now. But a little farther on he met two land crabs, scuttling along in the dust. "Get out of our way, pussy," they squeaked.

"Ho, ho, ho!" cried the cat in a terrible voice. "I've eaten five hundred cakes, I've eaten my friend the parrot, I've eaten an old woman, a man with a donkey, a king, a queen, his men-at-arms and all his elephants; and I'll eat you too."

And slip! slop! gobble! down went the two land crabs.

When the land crabs got down inside, they began to look around. It was very dark, but they could see the poor king sitting in a corner with his bride on his arm; she had fainted. Near them were the men-at-arms, treading on one another's toes, and the elephants, still trying to form in twos—but they couldn't, because there was not room. In the opposite corner sat the old woman, and near her stood the man and his donkey. But in the other corner was a great pile of cakes, and by them was perched the parrot, his feathers all drooping.

"Let's get to work!" said the land crabs. And snip, snap, they began to make a little hole in the side with their sharp claws. Snip, snap, snip, snap—till it was big enough to get through. Then out they scuttled.

Then out walked the king, carrying his bride; out marched the men-at-arms; out tramped the elephants, two by two; out came the old man, beating his donkey; out walked the old woman, scolding the cat; and last of all out hopped the parrot, holding a cake in each claw. (You remember, two cakes was all he wanted?)

But the poor cat had to spend the whole day sewing up the hole in his coat!

KING MIDAS and the GOLDEN TOUCH

In the old days there lived a king named Midas. Now this king had a good wife, a little daughter whom he loved dearly, and enough money to buy anything he wanted. And yet he was not satisfied. He wanted still more gold, for he was a miser and liked nothing better than to take out his gold coins and count them over and over.

One day while he was doing this, a voice said to him:

"King Midas, I have come from the gods and have been given the power to grant you whatever you most desire. But remember that you may have only one wish. What is it you would like to ask for?"

"What I wish," Midas answered at once, "is that everything I touch may turn into gold."

"You shall have your wish," the voice answered, "but I am not sure you will be happy with it."

When King Midas awoke the next day he touched his royal bed. At once it turned into shining gold. The golden sheets were so heavy upon his body that he hurriedly got out of bed.

He then picked up his slippers, and they too turned to gold. Later, when he went for a walk in his gardens, he touched the flowers and every blossom he touched immediately turned to gold.

"It is truly a wonderful gift I have," the King thought.

But when Midas sat down to breakfast, he was less certain about his gift. For, alas, no matter what he touched—whether the delicious fruit, the freshly baked bread or the glass of pure water—it all turned to gold. Suddenly Midas became frightened. How was he to keep from starving?

Just then his little daughter came running into the room. She reached up to hug him, and without thinking Midas put his arms around her. At once she turned into gold.

Poor Midas! When he saw that his daughter had turned into a gold statue, unable to move or speak, he began to weep. "Oh, my dear child!" he cried. "Whatever am I to do? What a foolish wish I made!"

The gods heard him weeping and took pity on him. The same voice Midas had heard before said:

"If you will go down to the river and wash your hands, this curse of gold will vanish. Then fill an earthenware pitcher with water from the river and sprinkle it over everything you have touched."

As fast as he could, Midas ran to the river and washed his hands in the fresh, pure water. Then he filled his pitcher and returned to the palace. The very first thing he did was to pour water on the golden statue of his daughter. At once the little girl was herself again, smiling and chattering as before. Then the King turned the food back into real food and ate it, and after that he turned the gold flowers in the garden into real flowers.

Never again did King Midas make the mistake of thinking that gold and money were the most important things in the world.

THE HUSBAND WHO TRIED TO KEEP HOUSE

There was a man so mean and cross he never thought his wife did anything right in the house. He could do more work in a day, he said, than his wife could do in three. One evening during the hay cutting he came home scolding and fussing and making more of a racket than usual because his wife was five minutes late with their supper.

"Dear love, don't be so angry," said his wife. "Tomorrow let's change our work. I'll go out with the mowers and mow, and you shall stay at home and mind the house and our child."

The husband thought this was a splendid idea. He was quite willing, he said, to make the exchange.

So early next morning the wife took a scythe over her neck and went out into the hayfield with the mowers and began to mow. And the husband stayed at home to mind the house and the child.

First of all, he decided to churn the butter. But after he had churned awhile he got thirsty, and went down to the cellar to tap a barrel of cider. Just as he was fill-ing his pitcher, he heard the pig come into the kitchen overhead. Off he ran up the cellar steps, with the pitcher in his hand, to stop the pig before it knocked over the churn. But when he got up he saw that the pig had already knocked the churn over, and was rooting and grunting while the cream ran all over the floor.

The man got so wild with rage that he completely forgot the cider barrel and ran at the pig as hard as he could. But the pig slid out of his hands and through the door. Then all at once the man remembered he had the pitcher in his hand. He ran back downstairs, but by the time he got there every bit of cider had run out of the barrel.

Then he went into the dairy and found enough cream left to fill the churn again. So he began to churn, for they had to have butter at dinner. When he had churned a bit, he remembered that their milking cow was still shut up in the shed, and hadn't had a bite to eat or a drop to drink all morning, though by now the sun was high in the sky.

He was afraid it was too far to take the cow down to the meadow, so he thought he'd just get her up on the housetop. The house was thatched with sods and a fine crop of grass was growing there.

Now their house lay close up against a steep bank, and he thought that if he laid a plank across to the back roof he'd easily get the cow up. But still he couldn't leave the churn, for the little baby was crawling about on the floor. "If I leave the churn here," he said, "the babe is sure to upset it." So he put the churn on his back and out he went.

But then he thought he'd better water the cow before he turned her loose on the thatch, so he took up a bucket to draw water out of the well. As he stooped to let the bucket down into the well, all the cream ran out of the churn and over his shoulders into the well.

Now it was near dinner time, and since he hadn't even churned the butter yet he thought he'd better boil the porridge. He filled the pot with water and hung it over the fire. When he'd done that, he happened to think that the cow might perhaps fall off the roof and break her legs or her neck. So he got up on the house

to tie her up. One end of the rope he made fast to the cow's neck and the other he slipped down the chimney. Running back down to the kitchen, he tied the rope around his waist. He had to hurry, for the water was now beginning to boil in the pot and he had not yet ground the oatmeal.

So he began to grind away. But while he was hard at it, down fell the cow off the housetop, and as she fell, she dragged the man up the chimney by the rope. There he stuck fast, while the cow hung halfway down to the bank. She was swinging between heaven and earth, for she could get neither down nor up.

The wife, meanwhile, had waited and waited and waited for her husband to come and call her home to dinner. But never a call did she hear. At last she thought she'd waited long enough, and home she went. But when she got there and saw the cow hanging in such a dangerous place, she ran up and cut the rope in two with her scythe. As she did this, down came her husband out of the chimney, and when his old dame came into the kitchen, she found him standing on his head in the porridge pot.

And that was the last time the husband complained about the way his wife kept house!

THE THREE WISHES

Many years ago there was an old man who had worked hard all his life to make a living out of his tiny farm. Though he made little money, he had a comfortable cottage, a strong donkey and plenty of food. But instead of counting his blessings, he sat with his wife before the fire one night wishing that he had some of the things that belonged to their neighbors.

"Instead of this little hut, which is on poor soil and only fit to house a donkey, I would like to have our neighbor's fine farm!" exclaimed the old man.

"While you are wishing, why don't you ask for their new house?" added his wife. "You might as well get as much as you can."

"And instead of my old donkey," her husband went on, "I would like to have the miller's young mule. My donkey isn't fit to carry an empty crate."

"Well, if I could have *my* wish," exclaimed his wife, "I would ask for a fine white horse with a silver harness. It seems as though some people have only to wish for a thing and they get it. How I should like to see *my* wishes come true!"

She had scarcely finished speaking when they saw a most beautiful little woman standing in front of the fire. This tiny lady could not have been more than eighteen inches tall, but on her head she wore a crown like a queen's. Her dress and veil were of such thin white material they seemed almost to be made of white smoke. And sparks from the fire jumped about her like fireworks, causing her dress to sparkle. In her hand she carried a golden wand with a gleaming red ruby at the tip.

"I am the Wishing Fairy," she said. "While passing by I heard your complaints, and I should like to help you. I have come to grant three wishes. One to you." She looked at the wife. "The other to you." She turned toward the husband. "And the third must be something you both want. I shall return at this time tomorrow and you can tell me then what the third wish is to be."

When she had said these words, the fairy sprang through the flames and disappeared in a cloud of smoke.

The delight of the old farmer and his wife may be imagined. How wonderful to have three wishes come true! They talked over all the things they wanted, but there were so many that they didn't know which to choose. Finally they decided to go to bed. Perhaps the next day they would be able to make up their minds.

In the morning they began talking about entirely different things, and shortly their conversation was once again about their wealthy neighbors.

"I was at their house early this morning," said the

husband, "and the cook was frying sausages. What a wonderful smell they made!"

"I wish I had a string of those juicy sausages in the skillet right now," said his wife.

No sooner had she spoken than there appeared on the skillet the most delicious-looking string of sausages that could possibly be imagined. The woman stared at them open-mouthed. But her husband jumped up in great anger.

"You foolish, greedy woman!" he cried. "What do you mean by using up one of our precious wishes on nothing but common sausages? What a silly goose you are! I wish that string of sausages was dangling from your nose!"

The words were scarcely out of his mouth when the sausages were actually hanging from the end of his wife's nose. She tried to pull them off, but they were stuck fast.

"Now see what you have done!" she exclaimed. "I may have made a foolish wish, but at least it hurt no one but myself. But you—just look at what you have done to me."

At that a swarm of flies came buzzing around the woman's nose, eager to get at the meat. In a rage the woman swatted at them, but they wouldn't go away.

"There is only one thing we can do now," she said. "We must use the third wish to get these things off my nose."

"Wife, for Heaven's sake! Think of the new house you wanted."

"What does it matter while I have this string of sausages hanging from my nose? These flies are enough to drive me out of my mind."

"Why not wish for a fortune?" her husband argued. "Then we could cover the sausages with gold and they would look beautiful dangling from your nose."

"Such nonsense!" his wife answered angrily. "I wish only to be rid of this thing, and nothing you say can make me change my mind."

At last the old man saw that his wife was absolutely set on this wish, so he agreed that their third request would be to remove the sausages from his wife's nose.

That night, when the fairy appeared and asked what their last wish was to be, they said:

"We wish only to be as we were before."

The fairy smiled and waved her golden wand. As she vanished again through the flames, the sausages tumbled off the old lady's nose. And the flies buzzed out of the house and were seen no more. From that time on, the old couple lived content with what they had, and there were no more wishes heard in *that* household.

THE THREE BILLY GOATS GRUFF

Once upon a time there were three billy goats named Gruff who lived high on a mountainside. There was not much to eat on their high pasture, but the mountain across the valley was rich in clover and sweet grass.

Now, to reach the other side of the valley the three billy goats had to cross a bridge. Under the bridge lived a wicked troll with eyes as big as saucers and a nose as long as a poker.

One day the youngest of the three started, *trip-trop,* across the bridge. At once the wicked troll shouted, "Who goes tripping over my bridge?"

"Oh, it is only I, the littlest Billy Goat Gruff," answered the little goat shyly.

"Fine! Then I shall come up and eat you!" said the troll.

"That would be foolish," said the littlest Billy Goat Gruff, "because I am so very little and I wouldn't make much of a meal for you. Wait for my bigger brother who will be coming this way soon."

The troll grumbled but he let the little goat cross over the bridge.

Not long afterward the second Billy Goat Gruff came *trip-trop, trip-trop,* stepping lightly on the bridge. "Who goes tripping over my bridge?" shouted the wicked troll.

"It is only I, the middle-sized Billy Goat Gruff," answered the second goat.

"Fine! Then I shall come up and eat you!" said the troll.

"Now that would be foolish, indeed," said the middle-sized Billy Goat Gruff, "because I am not so very big after all. Wait for my bigger brother who will be coming this way very soon."

The wicked troll grumbled but he let the second billy goat cross over the bridge.

In just a little while the third Billy Goat Gruff came *trip-trop, trip-trop, trip-trop,* trotting onto the bridge. He was so heavy that the bridge creaked and groaned under him.

"Who goes tramping and stamping over my bridge?" roared the wicked troll.

"It is I, the great big Billy Goat Gruff," answered the third goat.

"Fine! Then I shall come up and eat you!" shouted the troll.

"Come right along!" the great big Billy Goat Gruff shouted back.

The wicked old troll, not knowing what was in store for him, came hurrying up to the bridge. But the great big Billy Goat Gruff lowered his big strong head and tossed the old troll off the bridge and far down into the valley below. He was never seen again.

And the three Billy Goats Gruff ate to their hearts' content that day and every day, and lived to a great age.

PUSS IN BOOTS

There was once an old miller who was so poor that when he died he left nothing to his sons except his mill, a donkey and a cat. So the eldest son took the mill, the second son took the donkey, and the youngest son was left with the cat.

Quite naturally the youngest was sad that his share turned out to be so small. "What am I to do?" he said. "My brothers can make a good living by working together with the mill and donkey. But as for me, even if I were to eat my cat and wear its fur, I could very well die of hunger afterward."

The cat heard these words and looked up at his master.

"Don't worry, master," he said. "Just give me a bag and get me a pair of boots, and I will soon show you what a cat can do. You may find that I am worth more to you than *both* a mill and a donkey."

The young man doubted that the cat could help him, though to be sure his pet could do many unusual things. He had seen the puss hang stiff by his hind legs as if dead, and he had watched him catch mice in the most clever fashion. Without doubt the cat was a wise one!

So the young man got a bag and a pair of boots for the cat and told him to do whatever he liked. Puss drew on the boots and hung the bag about his neck. Then he took hold of the two strings of the bag with his forepaws and set off for a place where there were some rabbits.

Filling the bag with bran and lettuce, he left it lying open on the ground. Then he lay down, shut his eyes, and pretended to be sound asleep.

Soon a young rabbit smelled the food in the open bag and crept in. At once the clever puss jumped to his feet, drew the strings of the bag tight, and caught the rabbit.

Greatly pleased with his catch, the cat set off for the king's palace and asked to be allowed to speak to the king. He was taken into his majesty's apartment, where he made a low bow and said:

"Sire, I have here a wild rabbit which my master sends to you with his compliments."

"And who is your master?" asked the king.

"He is the Marquis of Carabas," said the cat, calling his master by the first name that came into his head.

"Tell your lord from me," said the king, "that I thank him and am pleased to accept his gift."

So Puss went proudly off in his boots, happy at the success of his plan. In a few days he hid himself with his bag in a cornfield. This time he caught two partridges and carried them to the king. The king sent his thanks to the Marquis of Carabas and gave the cat some gold coins as a present.

The cat went on doing this sort of thing for two or three months, and the king began to think that the Marquis of Carabas must be a famous hunter.

Now it happened one day that the king and his daughter were to take a drive along the banks of a river in a district where they had never traveled before. Puss heard of it and went to his master.

"Master," said he, "do just as I tell you, and your fortune will be made. You need only to go wash yourself in the river—at a spot I'll show you—and leave the rest to me."

The young man did as his cat advised, though he couldn't see what good it would do. While he was in the river, the king and the princess drove by, and the cat jumped out of the bushes and cried at the top of his voice:

"Help! Help! The Marquis of Carabas is drowning! Save him!" The king heard the outcry and looked out of his carriage. Recognizing the cat who had brought him so many presents of game, he ordered his coachmen to run to the marquis' assistance.

While they were helping the poor marquis out of the water, the cat quickly hid his master's clothing under a rock, then ran toward the king's coach in a state of great excitement.

"My master was bathing," he said, "and some robbers came and stole his clothes. I ran after them, shouting, 'Stop, thief!' but they got away. Then my master was carried into the deep water and would have drowned if you had not come by with your men."

When he heard this, the king commanded one of his servants to ride back to the palace and fetch some clothing for the marquis. They soon returned with a splendid suit which the king handed to the cat, who hastened with it to his master. So, at last, the Marquis of Carabas came up to the carriage, dressed much more finely than ever before in his life. The miller's young son, being healthy and well-built, was a good-looking fellow at all times, but now in his magnificent court dress he looked so stately that few, if any, of the young nobles could compare with him.

The king presented him to his daughter, the most beautiful princess in the land, and invited him to join the royal party in their drive.

Delighted to see that everything was going so well, the cat went on ahead. Coming to a meadow, where some men were mowing grass, he stopped before them and said:

"The king is coming this way. If he asks, you must tell him that this field belongs to the Marquis of Carabas, or you shall all be chopped into mincemeat."

When the carriage came by, the king put out his head and said to the men, "This is good grass land. Who owns it?"

"The Marquis of Carabas," they all said, for Puss had thrown them into a great fright.

"You have a fine estate, Marquis," said the king.

"Yes, Sire," the young man replied, tossing his head. "It pays me well."

Again the cat ran on ahead of the carriage until he came to some reapers. "Tell the king," he cried, "that all this corn belongs to the Marquis of Carabas, or you shall all be chopped as fine as mincemeat." The king, passing by a short time afterward, asked who was the owner of all the corn he saw.

"It belongs to the Marquis of Carabas," the reapers all shouted together, and the king again complimented his young friend.

The cat continued to run on ahead of the carriage, telling everyone he met to say the same thing. The king was amazed at the size of the estate of the young marquis. And the princess, sitting in her corner of the carriage, began to take more and more of a fancy to the handsome gentleman.

At last the royal party drew near the castle of the one who really owned all the fields they had passed through. Again the cat ran on ahead, and by asking questions he learned that the grand castle and all the land belonged to a wicked ogre, the richest ever known. From the servants Puss found out all he could about this monster—his riches, his power, his cruelty, and the many wonderful magical things he could do.

Then, saying he did not like to pass the castle without paying his respects, the cat asked to see the ogre. The monster received him politely—at least as politely as an ogre knows how—and asked him to rest awhile.

"I have been told," said Puss, "that you can change yourself into any kind of animal. They say you can even make yourself a lion."

"To be sure I can," said the monster. "If you don't believe me, watch, and you shall see me become a lion at once."

When Puss saw a lion standing before him, he was in such a fright he scrambled onto the roof. And there he stayed until the lion became an ogre again.

"That was dreadful!" said Puss. "Had I not seen it I would never have believed it. But it must be much harder for you to make yourself small. I have heard that you can turn into a mouse, but I don't believe it. That would be quite impossible."

"You don't believe it!" cried the monster. "Well you shall see!" And quick as anything he changed himself into a mouse and scampered about the floor. In a twinkling Puss pounced upon him and ate him up. And that was the end of the ogre.

By this time the king had reached the gates of the castle and thought he would like to see so fine a place. Puss heard the wheels and ran down just as the carriage drove up to the door.

"Welcome!" he said, as he stood on the steps of the castle. "Welcome to the castle of the Marquis of Carabas!"

"What! My lord Marquis," said the king. "Does this castle, too, belong to you? I never saw anything so fine. I should really like to enter."

"Your Majesty is welcome!" said the young man, bowing low and taking off the cap the king had given

him. Then he gave his hand to the princess, and they went up the steps. Puss danced before them in his boots.

Entering a great hall, they found a magnificent feast spread out. The ogre had been expecting friends for dinner, but they were afraid to come when they heard the king was at the castle. The servants, to whom the cat had given orders, quickly helped the marquis and his royal guests to all the good things on the table.

The king was amazed at all he saw, and the princess by this time was head-over-heels in love with the young marquis. When dinner was over the king took the marquis to one side, saying: "You have only to give the word, my lord, and you shall be my son-in-law."

Bowing very low, the miller's son accepted the honor bestowed upon him. The marriage was celebrated that very day with great pomp and festivity, and the happy couple lived to a good old age in the castle which had belonged to the ogre.

As for Puss in Boots, he became a great lord and needless to say, he never again had to catch rats or mice except for the pleasure of having a day's hunting.

The HARE and the TORTOISE

The hare was making fun of the tortoise.

"What a slowpoke you are!" mocked the hare. "Your legs are so short they never get you anywhere. Just look at my long legs!"

"Never you mind," replied the tortoise. "I can get places faster than you think. I'll be glad to run a race with you and prove it."

The hare laughed at the idea of running a race with the tortoise, but for the sake of a good joke he agreed. And he ran about the forest telling everybody how the tortoise had bragged that he could beat the hare in a race.

The day of the race arrived. The fox, who said he would act as judge, marked the distance and started the runners off.

The hare, of course, was soon far out of sight, but the tortoise did not care. He went slowly and steadily on his way.

After a while the hare grew tired. "I will take a short nap," he said to himself, "and show that tortoise just how ridiculous this race is." And after taking a drink at the brook, he lay down on the grass and fell asleep.

The tortoise continued to plod slowly and steadily down the road. He was hungry, but not once did he stop to eat. He was thirsty, but not once did he stop to drink. He passed many of his friends. He even passed the sleeping hare. But he never stopped. He just kept going steadily down the hot, dusty road.

Meanwhile the hare slept peacefully, never waking until the tortoise was almost at the goal. Then down the road the hare went, pell-mell, as fast as his long legs would take him. But it was too late. The tortoise reached the goal ahead of him.

Thus the hare learned that a race is not always won by the swiftest; slow and steady also does it.

TIT FOR TAT

There once lived a Camel and a Jackal who were great friends. One day the Jackal said to the Camel, "I know that there is a fine field of sugar cane on the other side of the river. If you will take me across I will show you the place. This plan will suit me as well as you. You will enjoy eating the sugar cane, and I am sure to find many crabs, bones, and bits of fish by the riverside, on which to make a good dinner."

The Camel consented, and swam across the river, taking the Jackal, who could not swim, on his back. When they reached the other side, the Camel went to eat the sugar cane, and the Jackal ran up and down the river bank, devouring all the crabs, bits of fish and bones he could find.

But being so much smaller an animal, he had made an excellent meal before the Camel had eaten more than two or three mouthfuls; and no sooner had he finished his dinner than he ran round and round the sugar cane field, yelping and howling with all his might.

The villagers heard him, and thought, "There is a Jackal among the sugar canes; he will be scratching holes in the ground and spoiling the roots of the plants." And they went down to the place to drive him away. But when they got there they found to their surprise not only a Jackal, but a Camel who was eating the sugar canes! This made them very angry, and they caught the poor Camel and drove him from the field.

When the men had gone, the Jackal said to the Camel, "We had better go home."

"Very well," said the Camel. "Jump upon my back, as you did before."

So the Jackal jumped upon the Camel's back, and the Camel began to recross the river. When they were well into the water, the Camel said, "This is a pretty

way you have treated me, friend Jackal! No sooner had you finished your own dinner than you must go yelping about the place loud enough to arouse the whole village, and bring all the villagers down to beat me with their sticks and drive me out of the field before I had eaten two mouthfuls! Why in the world did you make such a noise?"

"I don't know," said the Jackal. "It is a habit I have. I always like to sing a little after dinner."

The Camel waddled on through the river. The water reached up to his knees—then above them—up, up, up, higher and higher, until at last he was obliged to swim.

Then, turning to the Jackal, he said, "I'd like to roll over."

"Oh, pray don't; why do you want to do that?" asked the Jackal.

"I don't know," answered the Camel. "It's a habit I have. I always like to have a little roll after dinner."

So saying, he rolled over in the water, shaking the Jackal off as he did so. Thereupon the Camel swam safely ashore, but the Jackal was left to get back the best way he could.

The OLD WOMAN and the TRAMP

There was once a tramp who went plodding his way through a forest. The distance between the cottages he passed was so great that he had little hope of finding a shelter before the night set in. But all of a sudden he saw some lights between the trees. And then he discovered that they came from a cottage. No doubt there was a fire burning on the hearth. How nice it would be to toast himself before that fire, and to get a bit of something to eat. So he dragged himself toward the cottage.

Just then an old woman came toward him.

"Good evening, and well met!" said the tramp.

"Good evening," said the woman. "Where do you come from?"

"South of the sun, and east of the moon," said the tramp; "and now I am on the way home again, for I have been all over the world with the exception of this parish," he said.

"You must be a great traveler," said the woman. "What may be your business here?"

"Oh, I want a shelter for the night," he said.

"I thought as much," said the woman; "but you may as well get away from here at once, for my husband is not at home, and my place is not an inn."

"My good woman," said the tramp, "you must not be so cross and hard-hearted, for we are both human beings, and should help one another."

"Help one another?" said the woman. "Help? Did you ever hear such a thing? Who'll help me, do you think? I haven't got a morsel in the house! No, you'll have to look for quarters elsewhere."

But the tramp was like the rest of his kind; he was just as persistent as ever, and went on begging and praying like a starved dog, until at last the old woman gave in, and he got permission to lie on the floor for the night.

That was very kind, he thought, and he thanked her for it. "Better on the floor without sleep, than suffer cold in the forest deep," he said; for he was a merry fellow, this tramp, and was always ready with a rhyme.

When he came into the room he could see that the woman was not so badly off as she had pretended; but she was a greedy and stingy woman of the worst sort, and was always complaining and grumbling.

He now made himself very agreeable, and asked her in his most charming manner for something to eat.

"Where am I to get it from?" said the woman. "I haven't tasted a morsel myself the whole day."

But the tramp was a cunning fellow, he was.

"Poor old granny, you must be starving," he said. "Well, well, I suppose I shall have to ask you to have something with me, then."

"Have something with you!" said the woman. "You don't look as if you could ask anyone to have anything! What have you got to offer me, I should like to know?"

"He who far and wide does roam sees many things not known at home; and he who many things has seen has wits about him and senses keen," said the tramp. "Better dead than lose one's head! Lend me a pot, granny!"

The old woman now became very inquisitive, as you may guess, and so she let him have a pot.

He filled it with water and put it on the fire, and then he blew with all his might till the fire was burning fiercely all round it. Then he took a four-inch nail from his pocket, turned it three times in his hand, and put it into the pot.

The woman stared with all her might.

"What's this going to be?" she asked.

"Nail broth," said the tramp, and began to stir the water with the porridge stick.

"Nail broth?" asked the woman.

"Yes, nail broth," said the tramp.

The old woman had seen and heard a good deal in her time, but that anybody could have made broth with a nail—well, she had never heard the like before.

"That's something for poor people to know," she said, "and I should like to learn how to make it."

If she wanted to learn how to make it she had only to watch him, said the tramp, and he went on stirring the broth.

The old woman squatted on the ground, her hands clasping her knees, and her eyes following his hand as he stirred the broth.

"This generally makes good broth," he said; "but this time it will very likely be rather thin, for I have been making broth the whole week with the same nail. If I only had a handful of sifted oatmeal to put in, that would make it all right," he said. "But what one has to go without, it's no use thinking more about," and he stirred the broth again.

"Well, I think I have a scrap of flour somewhere,"

said the old woman, and went out to fetch some, and it was both good and fine.

The tramp began putting the flour into the broth, and went on stirring, while the woman sat staring now at him and then at the pot until her eyes nearly burst their sockets.

"This broth would be good enough for company," he said, putting in one handful of flour after another, "if I had only a bit of salted beef and a few potatoes to put in. It would be fit for gentlefolks, however particular they might be," he added. "But what one has to go without, it's no use thinking more about."

When the old woman really began to think it over, she thought she had some potatoes, and perhaps a bit of beef as well; and these she gave the tramp, who went on stirring, while she sat and stared as hard as ever.

"This will be grand enough for the best in the land," he said.

"Well, I never!" said the woman; "and just fancy— all with a nail!"

He was really a wonderful man, that tramp!

"If one had only a little barley and a drop of milk, we could ask the king himself to have some of this broth," he said; "for this is what he has every blessed evening—that I know, for I have been in service under the king's cook."

"Dear me! Ask the king to have some! Well, I never!" exclaimed the woman, slapping her knees. She was quite awestruck at the tramp and his grand connections.

"But what one has to go without it's no use thinking more about," said the tramp.

And then the woman remembered she had a little barley; and as for milk, well she wasn't quite out of that, she said; for her best cow had just calved. And so she went to fetch both the one and the other.

The tramp went on stirring, and the woman sat staring, one moment at him and the next at the pot.

Then all at once the tramp took out the nail.

"Now it's ready, and now we'll have a real good feast," he said. "But with this kind of soup the king and the queen always have one sandwich at least. And then they always have a cloth on the table when they eat," he said. "But what one has to go without, it's no use thinking more about."

But by this time the old woman herself had begun to feel quite grand and fine, I can tell you; and if that was all that was wanted to make it just as the king had it, she thought it would be nice to have it exactly the same way for once, and play at being king and queen with the tramp. So she went straight to a cupboard and brought out butter and cheese, smoked beef and veal, until at last the table looked as if it were decked out for company.

Never in her life had the old woman had such a grand feast, and never had she tasted such broth, and just fancy, made only with a nail!

She was in such a good and merry humor at having learned such an economical way of making broth that she did not know how to make enough of the tramp who had taught her such a useful thing.

So they ate and ate until they became both tired and sleepy.

The tramp was now going to lie down on the floor. But that would never do, thought the old woman; no, that was impossible. "Such a grand person must have a bed to lie in," she said.

He did not need much pressing. "It's just like the sweet Christmas time," he said, "and a nicer woman I never came across. Ah, well! Happy are they who meet with such good people," said he; and he lay down on the bed and went asleep.

And next morning, when he woke, the first thing he got was coffee and a biscuit.

When he was leaving, the old woman gave him a bright dollar piece. "And thanks, many thanks, for what you have taught me," she said. "Now I shall live in comfort, since I have learned how to make broth with a nail."

"Well, it isn't very difficult if one only has something good to add to it," said the tramp as he went his way.

The woman stood at the door staring after him.

"Such people don't grow on every bush," she said.

GUDBRAND on the HILLSIDE

There was once a man named Gudbrand whose farm lay far, far away upon a hillside, so they called him Gudbrand on the Hillside.

Now this man and his good wife lived so happily together, and understood one another so well that the wife thought her husband could do nothing wrong. And she was always pleased with whatever he turned his hand to. Besides their farm, they had a hundred dollars lying at the bottom of their chest, and two cows tied up in the barn.

One day the wife said to Gudbrand, "Do you know, dear, I think we ought to take one of our cows into town and sell it. Such well-to-do people as we ought to have spending money at hand like the rest of the world. As for the hundred dollars at the bottom of the chest, we mustn't touch that. But we really don't need more than one cow. Besides, we shall gain a little in another way, for I shall only have to look after one cow instead of having to feed and water two."

Well, Gudbrand thought his wife talked good sense, so he set off to town at once. But when he got there he could find no one who would buy the cow.

"Well, well, never mind!" said Gudbrand. "At the worst, I'll only have to go back home again with my cow. I've both stable and feed for her, and the road is no farther out than in."

But when he had gone a bit of the way, he met a man who had a horse to sell. Gudbrand thought it was better to have a horse than a cow, so he swapped with the man. A little farther on he happened on a man driving a fat pig before him. Gudbrand thought it better to have a fat pig than a horse, so he traded with the man. After that he went a little farther, and a man met him with a goat. Since Gudbrand thought it better to have a goat than a pig, he swapped with the man who owned the goat. Then he went on a good bit till he met a man with a goose, and he swapped away the goat for the goose.

When he had walked a long, long time he met a man with a rooster, and so he swapped with him too, thinking, "Surely it's better to have a rooster than a goose."

Then he went on till the day was almost over, and he began to get very hungry. So he sold the rooster for a shilling and bought food with the money. "It's better to sell the rooster than to die of starvation," he thought.

After that he went along till he reached his nearest neighbor's house, where he stopped for a chat.

"Well," said the owner of the house. "How did things go with you in town?"

"Rather so-so," said Gudbrand. "I can't praise my luck, nor do I blame it either." And with that he told the whole story from first to last.

"Ah!" said his friend. "I can see you'll catch it from your wife when you get home. Heaven help you, I wouldn't stand in your shoes for anything—going to market with a cow and coming home with nothing at all."

"Well," said Gudbrand on the Hillside, "I think things might have gone much worse for me, but whether I have done wrong or not I have so good a wife she never has a word to say against anything I do."

"I hear you saying that," answered his neighbor, "but I don't believe it."

"Shall we lay a bet upon it?" asked Gudbrand. "I have a hundred dollars at the bottom of my chest at home. Will you lay as many against them?"

Yes, the friend was ready to bet, so Gudbrand stayed there till evening, when it began to get dark. Then they went together to his house. The neighbor was to stand outside the door and listen, while the man went in to see his wife.

"Good evening!" called Gudbrand on the Hillside.

"Oh, is that you?" called his good wife. "So you're home safe, God be praised. How did things go at the market?"

"Oh, only so-so," answered Gudbrand. "Not much to brag of. When I got to town there was no one who would buy the cow, so I swapped it for a horse."

"For a horse," said his wife. "Well, that is a good idea. We are so well-to-do that we may as well drive to church just as other people do. And if we choose to keep a horse we have a right to get one, I should think. So run out, dear, and stable the horse."

"Ah!" said Gudbrand, "but you see I've not got the horse after all. For after I'd gone along a bit farther I traded it for a pig."

"Think of that, now!" said the wife. "You did just as I would have done myself. A thousand thanks! Now I can have a bit of bacon in the house to set before people when they come to see me. What do we want with a horse? People would only say we had got so proud we couldn't walk to church. Go out, dear, and put the pig in the sty."

"But I've not got the pig, either," said Gudbrand. "For when I'd walked a little farther, I swapped it for a goat."

"Bless us!" cried his wife. "How well you manage everything! Now I think it over, what would I do with a pig? People would only point at our farm and say, 'Yonder they eat up all they've got.' No, now I have got a goat, and I shall have milk and cheese, and keep the goat too. Run out, dear, and put up the goat."

"But I haven't got the goat any more than the rest," said Gudbrand. "For when I had gone a bit farther I swapped it away for a goose."

"Thank you! Thank you! With all my heart," cried his wife. "What would I do with a goat? If I had it I would lose half my time climbing up the hills to get it down. This way we can get milk and cheese from the cow as we have always done, and now I can have the roast goose I've been longing for. Run out, dear, and lock up the goose."

"Ah," said Gudbrand, "but I haven't the goose, either, for when I had gone a bit farther I swapped it for a rooster."

"Dear me!" cried his wife, "how you do think of everything just as I would have done myself! A rooster! Think of that! Now he'll get us up in the morning. As for the goose, I wouldn't know how to cook it. By all means run out, dear, and put up the rooster."

"But I no longer have the rooster," said Gudbrand. "For when I had gone a bit farther I got as hungry as a hunter, so I was forced to sell the rooster for a shilling, for fear I should starve."

"Now God be praised that you did so!" cried his wife. "What would we do with a rooster? We are our own masters, I should think, and can lie abed in the morning as long as we like. Heaven be thanked that I have got you back safe—you who do everything so well that I want neither rooster nor goose, goat nor pig."

At that Gudbrand opened the door and said, "Well, what do you say now, neighbor? Have I won the hundred dollars?" And his neighbor was forced to admit that he had.

RANDOM HOUSE BOOKS FOR CHILDREN

Question and Answer Books

For ages 6-10:
Question and Answer Book of Nature
Question and Answer Book of Science
Question and Answer Book of Space
Question and Answer Book About the
 Human Body

Gateway Books

For ages 8 and up:
The Friendly Dolphins
The Horse that Swam Away
Champ: Gallant Collie
Mystery of the Musical Umbrella
and other titles

Step-Up Books

For ages 7-8:
Animals Do the Strangest Things
Birds Do the Strangest Things
Fish Do the Strangest Things
Meet Abraham Lincoln
Meet John F. Kennedy
and other titles

Babar Books

For ages 4 and up:
The Story of Babar
Babar the King
The Travels of Babar
Babar Comes to America
and other titles

Books by Dr. Seuss

For ages 5 and up:
Dr. Seuss's Sleep Book
Happy Birthday to You!
Horton Hatches the Egg
Horton Hears a Who
If I Ran the Zoo
I Had Trouble in Getting to Solla
 Sollew
McElligot's Pool
On Beyond Zebra
Scrambled Eggs Super!
The Sneetches
Thidwick: The Big-Hearted Moose
Yertle the Turtle
and other titles

Giant Picture Books

For ages 5 and up:
Abraham Lincoln
Big Black Horse
Big Book of Things to Do and
 Make
Big Book of Tricks and Magic
Blue Fairy Book
Daniel Boone
Famous Indian Tribes
George Washington
Hiawatha
King Arthur
Peter Pan
Robert E. Lee
Robin Hood
Robinson Crusoe
Three Little Horses
Three Little Horses at the King's
 Palace

Beginner Books

For ages 5-7:
The Cat in the Hat Beginner Book
 Dictionary
The Cat in the Hat
The Cat in the Hat Comes Back
Dr. Seuss's ABC Book
Green Eggs and Ham
Go, Dog, Go!
Bennett Cerf's Book of Riddles
The King, the Mice and the Cheese
and other titles

Picture Books

For ages 4 and up:
Poems to Read to the Very Young
Songs to Sing with the Very Young
Stories to Read to the Very Young
Alice in Wonderland
Anderson's Fairy Tales
Bambi's Children
Black Beauty
Favorite Tales for the Very Young
Grandmas and Grandpas
Grimm's Fairy Tales
Heidi
Little Lost Kitten
Mother Goose
Once-Upon-A-Time Storybook
Pinocchio
Puppy Dog Tales
Read-Aloud Nursery Tales
Sleeping Beauty
The Sleepytime Storybook
Stories that Never Grow Old
The Wild and Wooly Animal Book
The Wizard of Oz

RANDOM HOUSE, INC., 457 MADISON AVENUE, NEW YORK 22, N. Y.